ORCA
YOUNG
READERS

Rescue Pup

Jean Little

ORCA BOOK PUBLISHERS

National Library of Canada Cataloguing in Publication Data

Little, Jean, 1932-
Rescue pup / Jean Little.

(Orca young readers)
ISBN 1-55143-299-4

1. Guide dogs--Juvenile fiction. I. Title. II. Series.

PS8523.I77R47 2004   jC813'.54   C2004-905170-9

Library of Congress Control Number: 2004112357

Summary: Shakespeare, a guide dog puppy who understands human speech, is placed for his first year of life with a foster child who has never learned to love.

Free teachers' guide available.

Orca Book Publishers gratefully acknowledges the support for its publishing programs provided by the following agencies: the Government of Canada through the Department of Canadian Heritage's Book Publishing Industry Development Program (BPIDP), the Canada Council for the Arts, and the British Columbia Arts Council.

Typesetting and cover design by Lynn O'Rourke
Cover & interior illustrations by Hanne Lore Koehler

In Canada:
Orca Book Publishers
1016 Balmoral Road
Victoria, BC Canada
V8T 1A8

In the United States:
Orca Book Publishers
PO Box 468
Custer, WA USA
98240-0468

07 06 05 04 • 6 5 4 3 2 1

Printed and bound in Canada.
Printed on 100% post-consumer recycled paper,
100% old growth forest free, processed chlorine free
using vegetable, low VOC inks.

*This book is for Autumn,
who in 1996-1997 raised a
Seeing Eye dog called Hula.*

*When Hula was two-and-a-half,
she became my dog guide.
I changed her name to Pippa since
I had trouble saying "Hula, heel" fast.
She did not mind.
She was the inspiration for this story
and its coming sequel.*

*Thank you, Autumn,
from the bottom of my heart.*

Table of Contents

Chapter 1

What's a Shakespeare?

The small yellow Labrador puppy who would one day be known as Rescue Dog was fast asleep on a heap of his brothers and sisters. One of his paws was hooked over his black button of a nose and one velvety ear was turned inside out. All the puppies had been battling tooth and claw ten minutes earlier. Now they were resting up before the next round.

Their mother raised her head, gave them a fond glance and started to doze off herself. Then her ears pricked up.

Someone is coming! she announced in Dog.

The next instant, the puppies caught the sound of approaching footsteps. They sprang to life, and Shakespeare was no longer top dog but a tumble of upended paws. He yipped in protest, but he didn't mean it. Such upsets were everyday happenings in the Seeing Eye kennels.

He was so busy collecting himself that he did not notice Jonah until the young man picked him up by the scruff of his neck and swung him through the air.

The pup kicked wildly. He hated dangling in space, especially when he was only half-awake. It was undignified and frightening.

Put me down! he yelped. *Put me DOWN!*

Jonah laughed.

How dare he? Shakespeare wished he could dangle the young man in mid-air and wave him around so he could learn how it felt. His paws scrabbled for purchase on Jonah's chest.

"This one's special, Meg," Jonah told the kennel girl at his side. "Has anyone explained his name to you?"

"Hold him properly, Jonah. You can tell he hates being swung around like that,"

Meg said. "I don't see anything special about him. He looks like all the others to me." She stretched out one hand to support the puppy's tail end.

"But he isn't. See his domed brow?" Jonah said. "Mary named him Shakespeare because his forehead reminded her of the great man's. She said he had an extra helping of wisdom. Some guy took her to see one of Shakespeare's plays the night before, and I think it addled her brain."

Meg peered at the puppy's head.

"That's crazy. He's sweet, but he isn't a Shakespeare." She laughed. "The others have almost the same shape of head. I'm forever having to check which is which."

"Almost—but not quite," Jonah said, finally putting one steadying hand under the pup's hind legs.

It was too late. Shakespeare wanted revenge. His dignity had been insulted. Jonah needed to be taught a lesson. The pup peed right down the front of Jonah's T-shirt. The young man yelled and put the puppy down fast.

"Blast!" Jonah muttered. When Meg giggled, Shakespeare felt sweet satisfaction.

The pup watched Jonah blush as the two young people left. Meg was still grinning. Shakespeare laughed. He liked her a lot.

Then he thought of what the two humans had said about him. What had it meant?

His sister Stormy pounced on him, ready to play, but he pushed her off. He wanted to know what the humans' conversation had been about. Mama would know. He trundled over and leaned against his mother's comforting bulk.

Mama, what's a Shakespeare?

What's a what? Mama said, nuzzling him fondly.

They said I was a Shakespeare, he told her. *What did they mean?*

It's your name, she said, staring at him. *You know your name.*

No. They gave me the name because of some other Shakespeare. Who is it?

Search me, Dearie, she said. *I speak Dog. You know I never was any good at understanding Human. People's talk goes in one of my ears and out the other. Except for important words like,* "Come," *and* "Quit that!" *I stick to Dog.*

Shakespeare stared up into her peaceful face.

You don't understand people? he gasped. He could not believe his ears. *I do,* he told her.

I've noticed that, she said. *And I know some of their language, of course.* "Good girl" *and* "No!" *The bits I need to get along with them. But that's it. Speaking Dog is enough for me. Most dogs don't trouble their heads with Human, son.*

Shakespeare stared at her. She must be teasing. He could not speak Human, of course—his mouth was not the right shape—but he understood almost every word humans said to each other. He did not know what a Shakespeare was, but he got most of the rest.

He turned to his brother.

Skip, what do you think a Shakespeare is?

No idea, Skip said through a yawn. *I don't listen to humans. They can't talk Dog. You are the only Shakespeare I ever heard of. It probably means dope.*

Shakespeare ignored the insult. He stared around at his other littermates. They looked as blank as Skip. None of them understood. He knew, suddenly, that they would not get it even if he tried to explain. He felt dizzy with shock. And, for the first time in his short life, he felt lonely.

I don't fit, he thought, gazing at his brothers and sisters. I'm not like them. I belong and yet, I don't. Is it something to do with my name?

He did his best to stay calm.

Tell me all the Human you know, he said to his siblings.

They glanced at him and went on playing. None of them wanted to bother thinking about language. In the end, he found out that they knew the same

6

bits and pieces as Mama, plus their own names.

That's all we need to know, Skip told him. *What's the use of learning a language we can never speak?*

Shakespeare tried to tell them that Human was fascinating. People moved their mouths, of course, which seemed silly. Dog did not need to be spoken aloud. It traveled from brain to brain with no trouble. It was easy and comfortable. Never surprising. Never a puzzle. Never the least bit exciting.

Human, on the other paw, was filled with interesting surprises. Jokes, for one thing. You didn't joke in Dog.

Dogs don't bother taking in much Human, Shakespeare, his sister Stormy told him in her uppity big sister way. *Just ignore their chatter, brother. If you want to fit in, you'll forget what you've learned. Thinking so much will give you an upset stomach.*

She was crazy. Shakespeare loved thinking and understood whole conversations between the people who came in and out of the kennels. He even got some of their jokes. He looked around at his family and felt sorry for them.

I'm lucky, he told himself.

All at once he no longer wished he were just like the rest. Even though he had no idea what good Human would ever do him, he could not give it up. He loved being bilingual. He enjoyed thinking like a person. He liked laughing too. Like all dogs, he smiled with his tail, but he laughed at Human jokes inside his head.

Hey, Shakespeare, let's eat, Skip said.

Shakespeare ran to get his share of supper. After all, eating was more important than talking, no matter which language you used. Food was the best!

Chapter 2

Meeting Stoneface

Shakespeare was chewing on his brother Skip's tail when Jonah and Meg came for him two weeks later. Giving up their daily fight to the death, the two pups joined the others and ran to say hello.

"Hi, guys," Jonah said. "Today's the big day for some of you. This very afternoon, Shakespeare and Skip are going to meet their 4H families."

"They're still such babies at eight weeks," Meg said. "It's hard to believe these two goofs will ever grow up to guide blind people."

Blind people? What were those? Shakespeare could not remember hearing of them before.

"Have faith," Jonah said. "I've seen pups like these grow up to work miracles. I'll bring Skip. You get Shakespeare."

Meg scooped Shakespeare up and checked the name on his collar. Holding him securely, she said, "These two are so alike I never know which is which."

"They were cut out with the same cookie cutter, that's for sure." Jonah grinned, leading the way. "Skip's going to a neat kid. He's already raised two dogs. Skip's lucky."

"How about Shakespeare?" Meg asked, troubled by his tone.

"They're sending the poor guy to the Bensons," Jonah told her. "Mrs. B. is great, but she's a foster mother who believes raising Seeing Eye pups helps her kids grow up. Some of the kids are rough and ready, to put it mildly."

"What do you mean?" Meg asked.

"Well, Shakespeare's going to her latest girl, Tessa. My sister goes to the same school. She says this Tessa is cold and stuck-up. At recess, when the teachers can't hear, the kids call her Stoneface."

"Stoneface! She sounds horrible," said Meg, hugging Shakespeare close.

Shakespeare shivered. Stoneface!

Feeling him tremble, Meg kissed the top of his head.

"Don't worry, boy. She'll adore you," she told him. "She won't be able to help herself."

Mushy, he thought, but he liked it.

Minutes later, she was passing him over to Martha. He and a black Lab pup called Larkin were put into cages and lifted into the back of a station wagon.

"Good luck, Shakespeare," Meg called, waving.

He longed to wave back. But they were driven swiftly away from the Seeing Eye kennels. The car splashed through a downpour and headed into the country.

I'm Larkin, the other dog said. *Who are you?*

I'm Shakespeare, Shakespeare said and waited.

Larkin gave no sign of having heard the mysterious name before. Shakespeare wagged his tail and sighed. Larkin and he would be friends, he was sure, but he could tell right away that Larkin, like Skip and Stormy, would see no point in understanding Human.

He turned his head and pressed his nose to the cage door. The breeze wafting in from the open window brought a feast of scents to his busy nostrils: gasoline, cows, rain, wet earth and the van itself. It was dizzying. He had never drunk in such rich scents. His nostrils quivered with pleasure.

Larkin whined from his cage, eager to make friends. Shakespeare sniffed back politely, but he stayed tense. They were in an alien world, and fascinating as its smells were, he did not know what was coming next. Other unexpected journeys had ended in the vet's office. And there was that Stoneface!

The car turned into a long lane. A big boy had turned in ahead of them. He glanced over his shoulder and broke into a run, ducking around some bushes and out of sight. Martha pulled to a stop before a farmhouse. A smiling woman opened the door. Martha opened Shakespeare's cage, snatched him up and dashed through the rain.

"This one's for Tessa," she said. "His name's Shakespeare."

"What a grand name for such a scrap," Mrs. Benson said with a laugh. "Hi, boy. You are beautiful."

Shakespeare stared at her, his brown eyes wide. Did all human beings know what a Shakespeare was?

Martha went back out and returned with Larkin. Mrs. Benson sat Martha down in a kitchen chair and sat down herself with Shakespeare on her lap. After petting him for a few moments, she glanced up.

"The kids will be home soon. How about coffee while we wait?"

"Wonderful," Martha said.

As the other woman put Shakespeare down, he heard a loud hiss from the top of a tall cupboard. A huge cat glared down at him.

"Stop that, Varmint," Mrs. Benson said.

"Does she live up to her name?" Martha asked, looking anxious.

"She adjusts in time," Mrs. Benson said, pushing the button on the coffeemaker. "She has survived twelve foster children and nine Seeing Eye pups. She has yet to inflict real damage—although they give her a wide berth."

My real name is Sheba, Queen of the world, and don't you forget it, pup, the cat said, growling at Shakespeare.

She sneered when the puppy showed his surprise.

Cats speak all languages so watch out, she said. *We even read minds.*

"How's Tessa settling in?" Martha asked, sipping the hot drink.

"She hasn't settled yet," the woman said slowly. "We've had lots of angry kids before, but Tessa's not just mad. It's as though she's locked herself in and can't find the key. We've had her since March, and she's still a tough customer. I'm pinning my hopes on Shakespeare."

They were almost finished their second cup when a sulky, string bean of a girl slouched in. *Slam!* That was the door shutting. *Thud!* That was her wet backpack hitting the floor. She jerked out a chair and plunked herself down on it. She kept her head bent and her face half hidden by a tangled mop of black hair.

Shakespeare sized her up. Big bark, no bite. He was sure of it. He bounced over to her, but her dark eyes were empty, and she turned away with no hint of a smile.

Shakespeare stared up at her. How could she not have noticed him?

"Where's Kevin?" her foster mother asked calmly.

"How should I know?" the girl said in a flat voice. She still pretended not to see the pup who was watching her so intently. "I'm not his babysitter even though he needs one. What's there to eat?"

Without waiting for the plate to be passed, she lunged forward and helped herself to a handful of cookies. As she jammed half of them into her mouth,

Martha gasped. The other woman did not bat an eye.

"Meet Shakespeare, Tessa," Mrs. Benson said, smiling. "He's eight weeks old and he's yours for a year. Isn't he a honey?"

"That's the dumbest name I've ever heard," snarled Stoneface, still avoiding looking at Shakespeare himself.

Her foster mother lifted the puppy and set him on the girl's lap.

Well, here goes, Shakespeare told himself. He was scared, but he was excited too. He wriggled and reared up to lick her chin. Even this frowning girl had to love him on sight. Everybody always had. But Tessa was not everybody. Before his tongue reached her face, she parted her knees and let him slither right through to the floor.

More confused than hurt, he lay in a startled heap for a moment. Then he scrambled up on his unsteady paws and began to pee.

Mrs. Benson grabbed him. She shot out the back door and deposited him on the

lawn. The grass was soaking wet, and he was through anyway. He looked up at her, tail drooping.

"I'm sorry, boy," she murmured. "You'll have to be patient. She'll be worth it in the end. I just know that girl has good stuff in her."

I sure hope so, Shakespeare said inside his head, but he cocked one eyebrow to show his doubts.

Mrs. Benson chuckled and gathered him up.

"We'll both have to work on her," she murmured into his ear, as though she, like Varmint, understood Dog.

She carried him back, nestled close in her arms. She sure was softer than the girl. Larkin watched Tessa from Martha's arms. He looked nervous.

Stone face, bone body, Shakespeare thought, pleased to have made a joke that sounded human. He looked at Larkin. *Relax,* he told his new friend. *I can handle her.*

Varmint was grinning at the puppy

puddle, which Mrs. Benson was bending to wipe up.

Baby, the cat said with a hiss.

The pup turned his face away.

Tessa laughed loudly. Not a real laugh. More of a bray.

Shakespeare flinched.

"Take him up and get acquainted," Peg Benson said firmly, putting the little dog back on the unwilling child's knees. "I wonder where Kevin is."

"I saw a boy going around the front as we drove in," Martha remembered. "Maybe he's already upstairs."

The girl stayed put for a minute, her face set. Then she rose slowly, holding the Lab pup out in front of her like a plate. Feeling insecure, he looked around for Larkin. Nobody was mentioning him. Shakespeare began to tremble again.

"Be gentle, Tessa," Martha said quietly. "He's only a baby."

Tessa ignored her. She tramped up the stairs, jarring Shakespeare with every step. At the top, she crossed a hall, put Shakespeare down on the floor, entered a room and shut the door in his face.

Chapter 3

"I don't want any dog!"

Shakespeare stared at the closed door. Nothing happened. He whimpered. Still nothing. She was in there, but she wasn't going to fetch him in to join her. Finally, not knowing what else to do, he threw back his head and howled.

Shakespeare's miserable wail sounded through the house. Tessa jerked the door open. She was not laughing now. Her eyes looked fierce. Scary even.

"Shut up, mutt," she hissed, glaring down at the puppy.

Shakespeare turned off his yowl and wagged his tail furiously. Tessa snickered in spite of herself. An instant later, she switched off her smile, but he knew it was still there inside her. He could see it gleaming in her eyes.

"If you ever dare make a racket like that again," she warned him, "I'll shut you up in my closet and keep you there on bread and water for a month."

Shakespeare cocked his head on one side and studied her. She could not really mean what she had just said. She must be a tease. He was one himself. He knew how it was done. He put one paw on her shoe, gazed up at her and made his tail go in a circle. That had always made Meg laugh. Tessa choked but refused to smile. She stared down at him as though he were a beetle or a worm. He cocked his head the other way.

"You are kind of cute," she muttered.

She stepped over his shrinking body, slamming the door behind her.

Shakespeare scratched behind his right ear and thought about her. Boy, she was mean! And he was supposed to soften her up. Fat chance!

Oh, I'll try, he told his shrinking self. I'm not a wimp. On the other hand, I have not even made it through the door to her room. But she had better show me she's human.

He cocked his head and listened for some clue as to where she had taken herself. A toilet flushed. Aha! Shakespeare did not understand what toilets were for, but they had them at the Seeing Eye. He lay on his stomach on the hall carpet and prepared to wait.

Crash! He winced as she stamped back into the hall. She did not look at him. She went straight to the bedroom.

Over her shoulder, she growled, "Get this. If I wanted a dog, you just might be okay. Not perfect but passable. But I do NOT want a dog. I don't want to care about anyone. It just ends up half killing you."

She shoved her way into the bedroom and left him outside again.

Shakespeare was about to despair when he saw that the door was slightly ajar.

She could have slammed it again, but she hadn't.

Being as quiet as it was possible for a puppy to be, he nosed the door open and crept through.

She was stretched out on the bed with her back to him. He stood and waited for her to turn over. When she did not, he ran around the bed and gazed up at her set face. Then he wagged his tail a little. A smile almost curved her lips before she remembered. She glared.

He wagged a little harder, bravely putting in a dash of joy. She kept her eyes closed, pretending she did not know he was there.

This was a game! He knew it. He padded over and put his paws up on the spread and gave a small yip of command.

"The Queen B said not to let you up on beds," the girl growled. Then she added defiantly, "But who cares what she says? She's not my boss. I can do what I choose."

As she leaned forward to haul him

up, Shakespeare flung himself onto her lap. He landed off balance and teetered wildly.

"Bad boy," she snapped. Yet, even while she scolded him, her hands settled him in a good position. He shivered with delight. This time, she was not going to let him fall.

"Don't shake," she whispered. "I never hit babies."

Her words acted like an off switch. The warmth ended. She threw her body backward on the bed and lay stiff, arms at her sides.

Now what? Shakespeare asked himself.

He took a deep breath and stretched to poke his cold button nose against her cheek. She did not respond. He licked her chin. She kept her eyes closed and her body rigid.

"Sloppy kisser, aren't you?" she muttered, refusing to play.

Shakespeare sniffed Tessa's hair and then her ear. She rolled away from his cold nose and wrapped both arms around her body in self-defense.

"I don't want you," she said. "I don't want anybody. No pets, no people."

Then the door burst open, and a large boy rocketed into the room.

"Hello, Stoneface," he sneered. "Has your pup turned you into mush yet? Has Ma Benson's magic wand transformed you into a Real Girl or are you waiting for Jiminy Cricket?"

Tessa sat up so fast she almost knocked Shakespeare flying. Meg had cut his nails before he left the Seeing Eye, but he dug what was left of his claws into the mattress and clung on for dear life.

"Out!" she said in a voice that bit a hole in the air.

"So you got a soppy little Lab, Messy Tessie," the wretched boy went on, staring at Shakespeare with what looked like hate. "I bet you adore him. You'll fall for Ma B.'s 'love a puppy, love a person' plan. You won't get to keep him though. Never forget that. He's only on loan."

"Beat it, Kevin!" Tessa yelled, pushing Shakespeare behind her. "You know you're not allowed in here. If you try it again, I'll personally smash your teeth in."

"You and who else," he mocked.

The lout was taller than she was, but flabby. He raced out the door when she, eyes flashing, leaped off the bed and charged at him.

Slam! She crashed the door shut in his face. Shakespeare winced and gave a low growl.

Now Tessa was the one shaking. She collapsed on the bed again. Had she forgotten him? He pushed against her and whimpered softly. Tessa gave him a dirty look.

"Kevin, are you up there?" Peg Benson called from the kitchen.

"We all have problems, dog. Don't be such a baby," she panted.

Only on loan, Shakespeare repeated to himself. What did that boy mean? He did not like the sound of it. Shakespeare hung his tongue out in a puppy grin. For the second time, Tessa's stony look gave way to a glimmer of a smile that was gone almost before he saw it. She stared at him, her dark eyes wide.

"Don't make me smile," she whispered. "I made a vow never to smile again until the world changes. You can't change the world for me."

Then she jumped up and ran to a desk and dug something out of a drawer. It was a snapshot of a smaller Tessa, holding a tiny kitten. Her face, bending over it, shone with tenderness.

"I found a stray kitten when I was six. I loved her so," she ground out. "One day, when I came home from school, she was gone. I thought she had gotten lost somehow and I searched and searched. Dad got sick of my crying and he finally told me she was dirty, and they'd found her a nice home in the country. Later my big brother Pete laughed and said they had just slowed down the car and dropped her in the ditch. He said cats lived on

mice and were fine in the country. But she wasn't a cat. She was only a kitten."

She choked back a sob and leaped off the bed again. She shoved the snapshot back in its hiding place. She stayed over by the window for a couple of minutes with her back turned to the watching puppy. Then she returned to the bed. Gazing up at her, he saw her face set like marble.

She flung herself down next to him without speaking. But now she was trembling. She couldn't be afraid of that punk, could she? He pushed his nose against her clenched fist, but it stayed tightly knotted.

Hey, Shakespeare said, whining. *Hug me. I'm so small, so lonely...*

Was it going to work?

She gave him a dirty look.

"Life is not easy for anyone, dog. Don't be such a wimp," she snapped.

She was stroking him though. Soon he would be eating out of her hand.

Then, downstairs, Larkin yelped. Tessa snatched up Shakespeare and ran.

Chapter 4

Runaways

Shakespeare knew that Larkin had not yelped in pain. He was just wildly excited. But Tessa dashed headlong down the stairs and skidded to a halt in the kitchen doorway. There sat Kevin, the lame-brained punk, with a goofy grin on his pimply face and Larkin in his arms.

"Kevin gave up his first Seeing Eye dog last month," Mrs. Benson told Tessa with a broad smile. "He said he didn't want to try again. Larkin has just made him change his mind. I had a feeling he would."

A man was standing there too. He had just come in, Shakespeare knew, because his hair and the shoulders of his denim jacket were wet. Tessa did not look at him. She went close to where the boy sat.

"Love puppies, love people," she murmured so Mrs. Benson could not hear.

Kevin scowled, but when Larkin gave a worried wiggle he grinned again.

"The puppy love part is okay," he said quietly. "I'll take better care of this one."

"Sure you will," the man said. "Tessa, aren't you going to introduce me to your new friend?"

The girl scowled and did not meet his friendly look.

"If you mean this dog, his name is Shakespeare," she muttered. "I'll take care of him if I have to, but he's not my friend."

"Well, he has a good name," said the man, coming over to stroke Shakespeare's head with one large callused finger. "I'm Dan Benson, boy. You can call me whatever you like."

Shakespeare raised his muzzle and licked the finger. He liked Dan Benson.

Kevin watched them, waiting for Tessa's reaction. She said nothing. She just jerked away from the man's hand and headed back to her room.

Winning her over was not going to be easy. Maybe it was not going to be possible.

But I won't give up, Shakespeare told himself. Not yet.

For the next two days, Stoneface did her duty by her Seeing Eye pup. She fed him and gave him water. She took him out to pee. She brushed him, although he wished that she wouldn't because she did not do it gently. Kevin was starting to act mushy over Larkin, but Tessa kept her distance and her cool.

Then, the third day Shakespeare was there, the kids took their pups for their first leash walk and got into big trouble.

It started as soon as they got out of sight of the house. Tessa began to run, jerking Shakespeare after her, showing off. Kevin hesitated and then began to yank poor

Larkin along in the same rough way. Neither of the puppies was harmed, but both were frightened. Shakespeare dug in his paws to brace himself, but Tessa was too strong for him. The next sharp tug made him turn a somersault, paws over tail. He let out a startled little yelp but was scampering after her again when she turned to look. Kevin laughed.

"He's an acrobat," he said.

"He's a clown," Tessa said coolly, but her pup heard the pride under the offhand tone.

Then they rounded the corner and forgot the dogs when they saw a bunch of kids playing softball in a school playground. Without thinking about it, both the Bensons' foster children stopped to watch.

"Awww, look at the puppies," a short girl in a red T-shirt shouted. "I say we take a time-out for saying hi to them."

The game was deserted while the half dozen players rushed to admire the small, bouncy dogs. Shakespeare and Larkin did their best to show off, jumping about and wagging their tails so fast they blurred. Yet Tessa's dog did notice that the kids spoke to Kevin and not his Tessa. Before he could do anything to help her, one tall boy looked up from stroking Larkin's ears.

"You guys, we're short a couple of players. How about playing?" he said.

"Yeah," chimed in the others. "Kevin can pitch."

"And I suppose I'll get stuck in the outfield," Tessa snapped. "We can't, not with the pups."

One of the girls said softly, "They're Seeing Eye pups, aren't they? I'm going to be raising one too."

"You're lucky, Autumn," another kid said. "My cousin raised one, but my mom says she's not raising anything but kids and roses."

Kevin ignored this. His face fell.

"That's right," he said slowly. "They're going to be Seeing Eye dogs. And we are responsible for them."

His disappointment was crystal clear. Tessa shot him a scornful glance. Then she shrugged her shoulders and did an abrupt switch.

"We can tie them to the fence for a few minutes," she said. "They'll be perfectly safe."

The girl named Autumn was gazing down at the two puppies.

"Do you really think you should? Maybe you ought to take them home first."

"I said they'll be perfectly safe," Tessa snapped, kneeling next to Shakespeare. "Mama B. will never know. These guys need us. Come on, Kev."

Kevin hesitated. Shakespeare could see him thinking that they shouldn't. But he badly wanted to play.

"You shouldn't leave them," Autumn muttered under her breath.

"They'll be all right," Kevin said, tying a sloppy knot in Larkin's leash.

In two seconds, the kids were deep in the game. They soon forgot all about their small Seeing Eye pups.

Larkin grew bored and curled up and went to sleep, but Shakespeare sat up and watched the game. He had been right. Tessa was doing a good job, but nobody spoke to her unless they had to. He waited for her to look over at him so he could show her how much he cared, but she never gave him a single glance.

At last, he too grew bored. He also felt neglected. He began chewing on his leash to put in time. Then he realized that he might be able to get Tessa's careless knot undone. It took a few minutes, but finally he got it loose. One end was still fastened to his collar, but he was free. It was great. He almost left without Larkin, but in the end he hadn't the heart.

Hey, Larkie, he said. *Want to come have an adventure?*

What? Larkin said through a yawn.

We can go exploring if you can get free like me, Shakespeare urged. *Hurry up.*

Larkin scrambled to his paws and did just what his brave new friend told him to do. Soon they were both free — even though they still had leashes trailing behind them. Shakespeare was in command.

Let's go, buddy, Shakespeare urged, and they took off. Their freedom went straight to their heads.

The two of them raced across the school-yard, squeezed under a fence and headed up the gravel road, which called out to them to come and see the world.

Zoom!

The first car just missed them.

That was close! Larkin said, staring after it.

Watch out, here comes… Shakespeare started to say.

His warning came too late. The second car came close to killing them both. It ran over Shakespeare's leash and knocked Larkin flying into the ditch.

Shakespeare rushed to sniff his friend. He lay still with closed eyes, but he whimpered softly. He was alive!

Get up, Shakespeare told him sharply.

Don't just lie there. Time is passing. We are on an adventure.

Larkin lay there, limp. Deep inside Shakespeare a coldness spread.

Larkie! Wake UP! he screamed in his top dog voice. *Don't just lie there. Open your eyes and get to your paws.*

He held his breath. Would it work? Was Larkin going to pull himself together? Shakespeare felt like a bully, but he had a feeling that if he didn't yell at his friend Larkie might never come back from wherever he had gone.

The other pup twitched and slowly, slowly stood up on all four paws. He looked dizzy, but he was doing his best to do what Shakespeare ordered. He staggered a bit and went in a circle. Then he moved his head back and forth to see if it still worked. His leash was gone. So was most of his nerve.

Shakespeare kept scolding and got him going at last. Running all out to set Larkin a good example, he glanced back to make sure the other pup was following him. He

was. He was unsteady, but he was trailing after his leader. Shakespeare was dizzy with delight. Never had he been free to go wherever he liked with the whole world to choose from. He was turning to face forward again, when all at once the earth beneath his feet dropped away, leaving him running on thin air.

Shakespeare yelped once and plunged head over paws into a swollen creek. The swiftly rushing water blinded him and filled his nose and mouth. He scrabbled desperately with his small paws, but there was no foothold anywhere. There was only the icy cold torrent, which knocked him about like a leaf or twig. It tumbled him over and over. He was choking. He was drowning. And he could do nothing to save himself.

Far away, he thought he heard Larkin howling.

Mama, help! his heart cried as a great darkness began to close in on him.

Chapter 5

Tessa Makes a Promise

Then a strong hand grabbed the scruff of his neck and hauled his small, battered body out of the jaws of death back into the sunny morning.

He tried to gulp in air, but he was still too full of water. The hands holding him turned him upside down and squeezed his aching chest. Creek water poured out of his mouth. He sneezed mightily three times. He coughed and retched. Then he began to breathe again.

"You poor little thing," a voice said.

The hands set him down on the grass. Loving the feel of solid ground under his paws, he shook himself. Creek water flew in all directions, spraying the girl and Larkin too.

"Poor baby," she said softly, picking him up again and wrapping his wet, shivering body in her warm jacket.

Then, out of the blue, Tessa and Kevin tore up, puffing and very red in the face. Kevin was silent, but Tessa was full of excuses. They sounded feeble to Shakespeare. His rescuer glared at his mistress.

"I think I should phone somebody about this," the girl said sternly. "You are living with the Bensons, am I right?"

Both children gasped. Kevin's cheeks paled, and he seemed to shrink. But Tessa straightened and looked the girl in the eye.

"We do live with them," she said, "but please don't phone. We'll take good care of our pups from now on. I swear. You'd get us in terrible trouble."

"You deserve to be in trouble," the girl said.

Kevin kept his head bent as he hauled off his T-shirt and struggled to dry Larkin off with it. Tessa was silent at last although she kept her chin up.

"Oh, all right. Promise me you'll look after them. They're so sweet," the girl said slowly. "What are your names? I'm Dorrie Wentworth, by the way."

"I promise. Solemnly. I'd sign in my own blood if you had a needle," Tessa vowed.

Then Kevin told her their names even though Tessa had not. The girl handed Shakespeare back, smiling into his eyes.

"Good luck, little one," she murmured and went on down the road. Tessa heaved a huge sigh of relief and instantly cheered up. Kevin, however, still looked glum.

"What's wrong? He's not hurt, is he?" Tessa asked gruffly.

"I don't think so—although he has some grease on his fur. The thing is, his leash is gone. Mrs. Benson made me swear I'd be careful. My last dog got away and met up with a porcupine and had to go to the vet to get twenty-two quills out of his mouth and nose. I promised never to let this one off the leash."

That was when Shakespeare found out what sort of girl his Tessa was underneath her tough shell.

"She'll be bound to find out because even if we get them dry they'll still smell. But I'll put Shakespeare's leash on Larkin and tell her my dog led yours into trouble. It *was* my idea so that's fair," she said.

When Kevin smiled, Larkin perked up too. They stayed outside until both pups were dry and had regained their bounce. Then the four of them went into the house.

"What happened?" Mrs. Benson asked at once.

"I don't know what you mean," Tessa began bravely.

"Never mind bluffing. You both look guilty as sin. Kevin has ruined his shirt somehow and I can smell the dogs from here. So tell us."

Mr. Benson winked at them.

"Might as well," he said. "She'll get it out of you in the end. And they smell like the creek."

Tessa stiffened as he started to speak. Then at his teasing words she gasped. She gave a shaky laugh and started talking.

Mrs. Benson did lecture the pair of them, but she picked on Tessa especially. Shakespeare guessed she could see how scared Kevin was that he'd have to give Larkin up.

"You mean the two of you just walked away without even looking back to be sure they were safe?" she stormed.

Shakespeare saw Tessa's brown eyes widen and go blank at this. What was it? He ran to her and put his paws up. She did not seem to see.

Mr. Benson changed the subject finally.

"You never told me you were interested in playing ball, Kevin," he said. "After the dishes are done, we could go out and see if you can strike me out."

Tessa snapped out of her trance and glowered at this.

"I'm a pretty fair pitcher," she announced coldly, "although you probably believe girls can't throw straight."

The man laughed. It was a deep, rumbling laugh that set Shakespeare's tail thumping the floor.

"No, Tessa," he said. "I just hadn't gotten to you yet. I know all about the power of women's pitching. Mrs. Benson and I met playing slow pitch, and the first thing she did was strike me out. She can come out and give us some pointers if she has time."

"Not today," his wife said. "That was long ago, Dan. Let's have some lunch. The children are probably ravenous after all they've been through."

Shakespeare watched Tessa, but if she was ravenous it didn't show. She was eyeing Mr. Benson as though she could not trust his kindness or his joking tone. She picked at her food and left half of it on her plate.

Maybe her insides were still aquiver with shock after his near drowning. He still felt very odd indeed.

When they went outside to practice pitching, Shakespeare was proud when

Tessa struck Mr. Benson out, but he had to concentrate or he was back in the creek fighting for breath.

In the warm kitchen, however, that fear was banished, replaced by his need to keep watch in case Varmint attacked him when nobody was ready to rush to his defense.

"He's only a baby, Varmint," Mrs. Benson said, staring at the cat who had just bristled like a bottlebrush and growled at the puppy. "What's come over that cat? She's never taken against a pup before, not like this."

Only Shakespeare knew the answer. Varmint had figured out that he understood Human. She had thought she was the only animal smart enough to do this. She would get rid of him if she possibly could.

Watching out for her kept him busy until bedtime.

As Tessa came in from taking him for his last pee of the day, she met Mr. Benson just outside the back door. He was looking up at the night sky. He put out his hand and caught her by the elbow. She tried to wrench free, but he held on and turned her so that she faced the same direction.

"Look at the moon, Tessa," he said quietly. "It is so lovely coming up between those pines."

Tessa pulled her arm away, but she also gazed at the picture he was giving her. Both of them, and Shakespeare who was listening hard, were astonished when she murmured, "Good night, moon."

"Where did...?" the man started and stopped, leaving the question unasked.

The girl stepped away, opened the door, and then in a low voice meant to be missed she said, "We bought it from the discard table at the library. When I was really little, Mom used to read it to me—until it fell apart."

"Oh, Tessa, I'm glad," he said. "We have it. Peg always read it to the small children they sent to us."

Tessa was almost out of earshot, but

she stopped long enough to pick up Shakespeare for a quick hug.

Then she dropped him and went up the stairs fast.

"Everything falls apart," he heard her whisper as they reached the upstairs hall.

That night, Shakespeare dreamed again that he was drowning. He was trapped under the covers and had no air to breathe. He thrashed around and yelped piteously.

Tessa shook him awake. "What's your problem, dog?" she demanded.

He was so happy to be rescued from his nightmare that he licked her all over her face.

"Stop it, you nut!" she hissed at him in a piercing whisper. "You'll wake up the whole house if you don't stop yammering. I don't love you, but you are safe with me."

He clambered onto her chest and tried to nip her ear. She twisted away and fended him off.

"Enough is enough, beast," she told him. "Go to sleep and BE QUIET."

Yet when she slept, he heard her whimper in her dreams. He stared at her dark shape in the bed. What was wrong? He did not know how to do it but he must find out and comfort her. She sounded exactly like a lost puppy.

Chapter 6

A Trouble Shared

Tessa was still at last, but the next night Shakespeare woke to hear her whimpering again. Soon her whole body shook with sobs. She woke herself this time and tried to muffle the sound by burying her face in the pillow. It did no good. Moments later, Mrs. Benson crept into the room. Shakespeare slipped to the floor, knowing by now that Seeing Eye dogs have no business sleeping with their mistresses. The woman ignored him. She sat down on the edge of the bed.

"What's the trouble, child?" she murmured.

Tessa wrenched her body away and

scrubbed at her wet face with the sheet. The tears kept coming. Her foster mother rubbed the girl's back and waited. Tessa wept on.

"Take some slow, deep breaths," Mrs. Benson said at last. "Crying eases the ache, Tessa, but it won't fix anything. Why don't you tell me what's hurting you so? It might not be as bad as you think. As my grandma used to say, 'A trouble shared is a trouble halved.'"

"Yes, it is as bad," Tessa sobbed. "I'm just like my mother. She sneaked out and got in a taxi and left without once looking back. I saw her from my bedroom window. And I left Shakespeare just the same way. I walked away, like you said, and he was nearly killed! If he had been, it would have been my fault. I was so bad my mother left and…"

She was crying too hard to go on.

Mrs. Benson waited for the storm to pass. Then she said quietly, "Now you listen to me, Tessa. Your mother's leaving was not your fault."

Tessa sat bolt upright and stared at her foster mother.

"How would you know?" she gasped. "You don't know a thing about it."

"But Tessa..." Mrs. Benson began, her voice gentle.

"Never mind. Go away. I don't want to talk to you." Tessa tried to thrust the woman from her.

Both Mrs. Benson and Shakespeare knew that she did not mean this. Shakespeare thought of his mama and longed to be back on the bed where he could nuzzle his girl. She needed him so.

"Even if I can't help, it's a good idea to bring hidden hurts out into the daylight where you can see them clearly," Peg Benson said calmly.

"My mother is dead," Tessa howled suddenly, "and I killed her. My dad said so. That's why he wouldn't keep me."

Mrs. Benson stood up. "I'm going to get you a drink of water and some tissues before you say one more word," she said, striding out of the room.

Quick as lightning, Shakespeare was up on his hind legs, scrabbling to reach his mistress. Would she notice him? Yes! She dropped one wet hand to touch the top of his head. He bounced at the hand and gave it his best kiss.

It wasn't your fault we ran off, he told her in Dog.

Then Mrs. Benson came back. When she handed Tessa a glass of water, Shakespeare watched his mistress gulp it down as though she'd just spent a week shut away from her water dish.

"Now tell me about it. And don't wander away from the facts, child. Your mother *is* dead, but the accident happened over a year after she left town. I cannot see how it can be your fault. I was told that you came into care months before word came that she had been killed in a car accident. She and a friend were headed this way, and a truck went out of control and smashed into their vehicle. Your mother wasn't even driving when it happened. How could her death be your fault?"

Once again, Tessa jerked upright and stared. "What did you say?" she whispered.

Peg Benson repeated herself in a quiet, steady voice and handed Tessa another tissue.

"My father told me that she killed herself right after she left," Tessa said. She sounded as though every word was choking her. "He was in a rage. He shouted that if I had been a better girl... Then my brother dialed 911 and they came and got us."

Mrs. Benson broke in. "Well, he was lying. That is simply not true, Tessa. Your mother's death had nothing whatsoever to do with you."

"Maybe you're the one who's lying," Tessa said raggedly. "How do you know so much anyway?"

"I make a point of learning all I can about every new child I foster. Why would I lie? I am so sorry you were not told, but you know your father was a violent man. Both your brothers refused to return to his care, even when he applied for custody."

Tessa fell back and put her arm across her face. Seeing her shoulders heave, Shakespeare made a wild scramble to get to her and landed back on the floor with a thump. Mrs. Benson laughed softly and lifted him onto her lap.

"You are upsetting your pup," she said.

"But I *am* bad," Tessa whispered. "Shakespeare almost drowned because of me."

"Tessa, Tessa, stop it. Shakespeare is right here, very much alive. I know he's going to be up on your bed the minute I'm gone so you might as well take him now. Dogs can be very comforting."

"But Shakespeare did nearly die," Tessa insisted in a small voice, gripping her foster mother's arm. "I wasn't watching... If he *had* died..."

"I must tell you sometime about the day I nearly killed our very first foster child, John. He hid in the dryer. He yelled just as I reached to turn it on. Now, no more melodrama! Here's your dog. It's time to get to sleep."

Shakespeare scrambled into his girl's waiting arms and went to work on her tear-streaked cheeks. Mrs. Benson was almost out the door when Tessa said softly, "Thanks ... Mrs. B."

The woman paused for a second and glanced back.

"You're welcome, honey," she said gently.

Shakespeare glimpsed a shadow waiting in the hall. As Mrs. Benson started to leave the room, Mr. Benson looked in.

"You get to sleep now, Tessa, or we'll be up all night worrying about you," he rumbled.

Tessa hiccuped. "Yes, sir," she got out, halfway between a sob and a laugh.

She only spoke once more.

"She was heading back," she whispered to herself. "Maybe she was coming for me after all."

The next day, Tessa had a long talk with her foster parents. Shakespeare dozed at her feet. The blank look that he had seen in her eyes was gone most of the time.

"We're going to see a therapist," she confided in him. "I get to take you with me. I told them I wouldn't go without you."

Mrs. Belle was kind. When Shakespeare smelled two Wheaton terriers on her ankles, he relaxed. Tessa took a while to get started talking, but before long she poured out all her mixed-up feelings. Mrs. Belle was almost as good a listener as Shakespeare himself.

They had gone to see her twice when it was time for the kids to take their pups to their first 4H Puppy Raisers meeting.

On the way, Shakespeare saw that Tessa was growing stiff and distant.

No, he thought. Not Stoneface again. And he began to plan how to keep her from putting on that mask.

Chapter 7

Autumn

Several boys and girls of varying ages sat in a circle, each with a pup at his or her feet. Tessa sat down beside an empty chair. To Shakespeare's delight, one of the puppies was his brother Skip. The boy raising him was the younger brother of Dorrie Wentworth, the teenager who had pulled Shakespeare out of the creek. She was helping run the group. When Tessa spotted her, the color drained from her face and she gasped. Shakespeare knew she was wondering if Dorrie would tell what had happened.

"I'm Dorrie Wentworth," she said. Then she gave a special grin to Tessa and Kevin.

"I thought we'd meet again," she went on. "I'm glad to see that you kept your word."

Tessa slumped in relief.

Then another girl rushed in with her pup bouncing ahead of her. It was Autumn from the softball game. She slid into the empty chair and mumbled that she was sorry for being late.

"We're just going to start," Dorrie said, giving her an encouraging smile. "Catch your breath, Autumn."

Then an older lady talked about the importance of what they were doing. Shakespeare worried about his girl. The rest looked eager, but she was stiff, her face wooden.

Autumn's dog was a yellow Lab named Hula. Shakespeare thought he remembered her, but he was not sure. He stretched out his paw and rested it on the girl's foot. She shifted. He waited a moment. Then he did it again. Tessa noticed.

"Sorry," she said gruffly, leaning over to move her dog.

"It's okay," Autumn said with a friendly smile. She did not seem to notice Tessa's coolness. "Hula's my first Seeing Eye pup. Have you raised others?"

"No," Tessa replied. "Shakespeare's my first too."

"Is his name really Shakespeare? Like the writer?" Autumn whispered.

"Is her name really Hula? Like the hoop?" Tessa shot back, her face deadpan.

They smothered laughter. Then Autumn said, "I remember you the day we played ball at the school. I was worried the pups would escape. I'm glad they weren't hurt."

Tessa went rigid. "They almost died," she got out. "I bet Dorrie told everybody. She had to pull Shakespeare out of the creek."

"I didn't know," Autumn said, her eyes wide.

"I'll just bet," Tessa growled, jerking her body around so she had her back to the other girl.

From that moment on, she stayed cold and shut off, Stoneface to the life. There was nothing Shakespeare could do. He soon realized that Hula was nearly as smart as he was, although he did not think that she could understand Human. But Tessa never let him get close enough to Autumn and her dog to find out. Whenever they got up, she waited until the other girl sat down, and then she headed for an empty chair as far away as she could get.

After two days of this, Shakespeare was growing desperate. How on earth could he get through to her that Autumn was innocent—and confused?

Then, on the third day, it was not Peg Benson but her husband who waited outside to take Tessa home. Kevin asked permission to go off with another kid and left. Tessa and Mr. Benson started for home. Halfway there, the man pulled off the gravel road and stopped the car.

"What's the trouble, Tessa?" he asked quietly.

"I don't know what you mean," Tessa said, staring out the window.

"Sure you do," he said, a smile in his low voice. "I think you've got off on the wrong foot somehow, and you don't know how to fix it. Am I right?"

Tessa did not speak. Shakespeare wagged wildly, doing his level best to say, "Yes!"

"Well, I've lived a lot longer than you have, so I've done it myself. Put my foot in my mouth and got it stuck. So here's my advice for what it's worth. Stretch out your hand and use your smile. The foot will come loose. When it slides out, try saying you don't know what came over you, but you'd like to start over. How about it? Then wait. I bet it'll work out."

Tessa still would not speak, but her shoulders had relaxed. Shakespeare saw, suddenly, that she was crying. They were good tears though.

The car started up, and they were at home in five minutes. The girl jumped out. Then she hesitated, swiping the tears off her cheeks.

"Maybe…I'll try."

When the two of them walked in to the class the next morning, Shakespeare was afraid she would not be able to go through with it. She glanced sideways at Autumn and stalled. But her puppy was having none of that. Small as he was, he dragged his girl to the empty chair beside Autumn. Tessa sat down with a bump.

"Hi," Autumn said without looking at her.

"Hi," Tessa responded, her cheeks red. "I'm sorry I was so…I got kind of mad or something. I don't know why…"

"Forget it," Autumn said, grinning at her. "Everybody gets off on the wrong foot sometimes."

"That's just what my…my dad said," Tessa answered.

"All right, you two, time to stop chattering and get to work," said the lady in charge.

And Shakespeare and Hula hit it off at once. Shakespeare knew right away just what to do, and before long not only Larkin but Hula too was copying him.

"Ours are by far the smartest," Autumn whispered just as Hula got fed up with being good and rolled onto her back, waving her paws in the air.

"I can see that," Tessa said dryly.

"Hula, stop acting like a prize idiot," Autumn wailed, but she could not help laughing. Hula was definitely a clown.

By the end of the meeting, the two girls were almost friends. Mr. Benson was waiting for them. Tessa had begun trying to call her foster parents Mom and Dad but it was still hard. She looked away and went for it.

"This is Autumn, Dad," she said, not meeting his eyes.

"Hi, Autumn," Dan Benson said, giving Tessa's shoulder a squeeze. "It looks as though your dog and my daughter's dog are best friends."

"That's for sure," Autumn said with a big grin at Tessa.

Tessa looked startled. She smiled back uncertainly.

She will get used to being liked,

Shakespeare thought, pleased with how things were progressing. Her face didn't look as blank as a hard-boiled egg anymore.

Then, six weeks later, it was announced that the next 4H group was to meet at Autumn's place.

"We must remember to pen up Zorro before you come," Shakespeare heard Autumn mutter. "He does not like dogs. Even Hula is afraid of him."

"Who's Zorro?" Kevin asked.

"Our attack rooster. He's meaner than mean. I'll shut him up with the hens."

"Don't worry," Tessa said. "Shakespeare won't be scared by a mere rooster."

"You don't know Zorro," her friend said. "He's a menace. Even my dad is scared of him."

Tessa grinned. Surely Autumn was kidding.

The next day, Mrs. Benson drove Shakespeare and Tessa to Autumn's house a little early. When Tessa closed the

car door and turned to go to the house, Zorro, forgotten by Autumn, spotted the puppy. Shakespeare did not see the rooster coming until he attacked.

His wingspread was enormous. He made a mad cackling noise. His small eyes were bright with menace. His head, with its lethal beak, drew back and stabbed at Shakespeare's face. A four-month-old puppy was no match for an enraged rooster. Shakespeare shut his eyes tight and cowered against his mistress. For the second time in his short life, he believed he was about to die.

Tessa swore loudly at the bird and flapped her arms. But Mrs. Benson saved the day. She blasted the car horn. Zorro, startled and distracted, flapped backward for an instant. Autumn's dad ran up and dove for him before he could recover. Throwing an empty feed sack over him, he bundled up the furious bird and bore him away.

"I'm so sorry, Tess," Autumn cried. Tears were running down her cheeks.

Tessa was pale and shaken, but she grinned at her friend. "If he'd hurt my dog, I'd have killed him," she said matter-of-factly.

Autumn's father turned his head in time to hear this.

"We'll eat him instead. It'll be justifiable homicide," he said, his face and voice grim.

"Eat Zorro?" Autumn gasped, staring up at him.

"He'll taste like any old chicken, only tougher than most," her father said. "We'll call the next one Cocky-Locky. No more attack roosters."

After the meeting of the puppy raisers finished, Kevin went off with Autumn's brother Nick.

"Your mom says you can stay for a couple of hours," Autumn said. "Would you like to? She said to phone to tell her what you decided."

She sounded unsure of Tessa's answer. Shakespeare longed to tell Autumn that Tessa was not really Stoneface. He went over to Hula and wagged his tail to show his mistress how easy it was to make friends.

"Hula thinks that dog of yours is her boyfriend," Autumn said, giggling.

Tessa had begun to stiffen up, ready to be hurt. Then she saw her dog looking up at her as if he were trying to give her a message. The look felt like a nudge in the ribs. Her eyes widened as she took in the anxious yet hopeful look on Autumn's face.

She wants you to say yes," Shakespeare thought. Get with it!"

Would she get the message?

"If Mrs. B. says it's okay, I'd like to stay," Tessa said.

Autumn gave a bounce of pure pleasure. "Great. Come on up to my room," she said, clattering up the stairs.

They spent time talking about everything from their favorite singers to their favorite characters in *The Lord of the Rings* and in the *Harry Potter* movies. Autumn had all the books and loaned Tessa a couple.

"I can really get my mother going by saying I like Draco Malfoy best," she confided. "She's scared I admire his evil ways. He is really handsome though."

"I told Mrs. B. I like Gollum," Tessa said, laughing. "But she just said she thinks he's 'preciousss.'"

Hula was dozing on her special mat in the corner. They had examined Shakespeare to make sure he was undamaged after Zorro's attack. He seemed unhurt. Now he lay stretched out on Autumn's bedside rug, looking totally at peace. But nobody could see the scars left by fear.

That night, in his dreams, evil birds drove him into the dark rivers that already filled his nightmares. He woke Tessa twice. She didn't let him up on the bed now. She understood why she shouldn't. She took her pillow and lay next to him on the floor and petted him until he calmed down. She told him things he did not understand but tucked away in his memory.

"When you're a dog guide," she said, "you may stay in hotels with your blind person, and they would not like a dog on the bed there. Whatever is bothering you, forget it and sleep. I will keep you safe."

Wondering what a hotel was helped him forget roosters and drowning.

Chapter 8

Snow

The Seeing Eye pups learned a lot in the months that followed:

Don't pee in the house.

Don't bark.

Don't jump on the beds or the people.

Don't eat the shoes, the chair legs,
  the plants, the socks.

Don't drag dirty underwear into
  the living room.

Don't chew up Grandma's hearing aid.

Come when they say, "Come."

Sit when they say, "Sit."

Back away when they say, "Leave it!"

"Shakespeare is brilliant," Tessa bragged. "I only have to explain a thing once and he gets it."

"Larkin's smart too," Kevin said.

Shakespeare looked down so nobody would catch the laughter in his eyes. Larkin was smart. He was smart because as soon as Shakespeare heard what Tessa had in mind, he translated it into Dog. He helped Hula out too, although she was pretty quick. Skip ignored him. After all, Shakespeare was his brother, not his teacher.

We make a great pair, Larkin said. *I'm so glad we're together. I'm more like your brother than that pup, Skip.*

The poor sap thought he was Kevin's for keeps. But Shakespeare had been eavesdropping. He knew they were going to be taken away someday. They had to help blind people. He still was not quite clear what a blind person was or how he and Larkin could help one, but he was certain they were not going to stay at the Bensons all their lives.

Then something happened that made Shakespeare forget everything else.

He woke up one morning to hear Tessa crying out, "Oh, it's snowing!"

Kevin opened the door wide, and the kids stood laughing as their half-grown pups tumbled out into the white stuff. They snuffled in the snow collecting by the fence and blowing in the wind. The first flakes melted and so did the second and third, but then a day came when it stayed and even got almost deep. That was when the real fun began.

After the first morning, Shakespeare and Larkin would burst out the door the moment it was opened for them and roll and roll. It felt so good. Then they would chase each other and the children around in the side yard where the drifts piled highest.

When snowballs whizzed through the air, the two pups would dash to catch them and, when they almost managed it, would be shocked by a cold wet face full of snow.

"They never learn," Tessa said, laughing and tossing one for her pup to go after.

Shakespeare really had learned, but he loved the running and jumping to try to capture the flying handfuls. He loved Tessa's gleeful shrieks when he shook his head and ears and created a little snow-storm of his own.

Then Christmas came, and the family hung up stockings for the pups. They got chew sticks and balls and a big rope each. They also were given enormous marrow-bones. The only trouble was that Mrs. Benson took the bones away just when they were getting truly delectable.

"You've sucked out all the marrow," she said. "Next thing, you'll break them and swallow a sharp splinter, and I will never be forgiven."

As part of their training, they went to the library.

"Oh, look!" Tessa cried out in delight. "There's a picture of Shakespeare. Look, boy. That's the man you were named after. He wrote plays."

Shakespeare peered up at the black and white sketch of the balding playwright. Was he the answer to the mystery? He did have a tall, domed forehead.

"He was brilliant, just like you," the girl added, petting her pup. Shakespeare smiled at the face on the wall and told himself he would remember.

The kids took their puppies on the bus. They even went to Sunday school and were introduced to the younger children at story time.

At home, Larkin got in big trouble for stealing a drumstick, and Shakespeare got in even bigger trouble when he got out the back door long enough to meet a skunk who had come out of hibernation and was exploring the vegetable garden.

I was just being friendly, he told them as they gave him his third bath.

He made up for the skunk incident a week later.

"Sometimes the snow never gets deep enough for tobogganing," Dan Benson said. "But this Saturday it is going to be perfect."

"Can the dogs come?" Tessa asked, scratching Shakespeare's ear.

"We'll take them, but if they get out of the car somebody will have to hold tight to their leashes, or one of you could get hurt," Mrs. Benson said.

They had a glorious time. They were all heading back up the hill and Tessa had leaned over to dust off the snow on her pants when Shakespeare saw another toboggan careening straight for her. He could have barked a warning, but he was not sure she would get the message fast enough. So Tessa's dog jerked the leash out of Mrs. B.'s hand, jumped at Tessa and sent her and himself sprawling into a deep drift. The toboggan shot past. She sat up and watched it thunder on by. Kevin charged over to make sure she was all right.

"I thought you were a goner, Tess," he panted.

"Me too," Autumn gasped. "I wonder if

Shakespeare knocked you out of the way on purpose."

"He certainly did," Peg Benson said. "He nearly jerked my arm off in the process. Good boy, Shakespeare!"

Tessa knelt in the snow and hugged her pup close.

"He's a rescue dog," she said. "Like those Saint Bernards who save skiers who get injured or lost in the snow in the Alps."

"Is there a little keg of brandy under his chin?" Autumn's father asked, pretending to look. "If so, it's mine."

Shakespeare had never heard of those dogs, but he knew his heart was still thumping. He did not think he would want the job of saving lost people.

Are those blind people we are going to help lost? he asked Tessa.

But she did not read his mind and nobody explained.

When they got home and told the story to Mr. Benson, he eyed Shakespeare thoughtfully.

"He's special somehow," he said at last.

"We've had kids raise a dozen pups in this house, but he's got an added something about him."

"He understands everything," Tessa said softly. "If he could talk, you'd see. He even gets my jokes."

Kevin grinned at Shakespeare.

"Knock, knock," he said.

"Who's there?" Mr. Benson obliged, pretending to speak for the dog.

"It's … um … dog," Kevin said.

"Dog who?" asked Mr. Benson.

Before Kevin could answer, Tessa put in. "Dog the best, dog the smartest and dog my darling!"

"Hey, I'm doing it!" Kevin yelled at her.

"Okay. Dog who?" she asked.

"Dog gone dope," he said.

Everyone laughed, but Tessa whispered into her pup's floppy ear, "My answer was the truth."

The dogs grew bigger and stronger, but Shakespeare was still careful to draw back whenever Tessa went near the creek.

Autumn came over often with Hula.

"Hey, Shakespeare, would you like to come and see Zorro?" she teased Tessa's dog, even though Zorro was long gone.

Shakespeare could not help shuddering every time he heard the rooster's name. Even Tessa had to smile at his anxious look.

Winter drew to an end. The snow melted away. The day when they must say good-bye would come soon, Shakespeare guessed. Tessa spent more and more time with her arms wrapped around him, whispering into his soft ears how much she loved him. He did his best to ignore his growing heartache, but it was hard to do. He could not imagine getting through the days without her. They planned their every move together and faced each new challenge as though the two of them were one being.

But one day the phone rang.

"That was Martha," Mrs. Benson said. "She'll be coming over sometime in the next couple of weeks."

Tessa stiffened, and her dark eyes went wide.

"Martha who?" Kevin asked. He and Larkin were lying on the floor making something complicated out of Lego.

"Martha from the Seeing Eye. She wanted my hermit cookie recipe. But she reminded me that it is almost time for the pups to go back to the Seeing Eye and start their training as dog guides. She promised to call before she comes."

Shakespeare felt Tessa's fingers dig into his back as if she would never, ever let him go. He twisted his head around and kissed her arm. If only he could do one grand thing for her before he left. With so little time to go, how would he ever manage it?

Chapter 9

Dream Come True

A week later, Shakespeare overheard Martha's call to say she was coming for them.

"Next Friday morning? I'll write you in on the calendar," Mrs. Benson said with a catch in her voice.

They had arrived on a rainy afternoon in May and May had come around again. Although today was clear, the night before there had been a surprisingly violent thunderstorm. Shakespeare usually did not show he was worried during storms, but this one had scared him.

"It might have been a hurricane," Kevin said.

"And it might have been a typhoon," Mr. Benson teased.

"Personally, I thought it was a tornado," Tessa put in.

The next morning, Kevin and his dog went on a Scout hike. After they'd gone, Mr. Benson invited Tessa to come for a walk in the woods.

"I want to see if any of the old trees are damaged," he said.

The man and girl walked together in a comfortable silence while Shakespeare dashed about on his leash, snuffing up fresh scents, reveling in all the smells that he had forgotten since last spring.

Mr. Benson broke the silence.

"I'm proud of you, girl," he said, pausing by a giant maple. "You're a long way from the Tessa who came banging into our place a year ago. The chip is off your shoulder, and there's a wonderful smile on your face."

Shakespeare saw Tessa blush and knew she was pleased. She glanced sideways at Mr. Benson and tried to think of just the right words to say. Then she saw Shakespeare with his nose in a pile of wet leaves and laughed.

"Look at him," she said, giggling. "He looks like he's sniffing fresh bread or pizza."

"It smells like heaven, doesn't it, boy?" Dan Benson said, chuckling.

But he sounded absent minded, as though he were thinking about something else. Both Shakespeare and Tessa turned their heads to look at him, their eyes filled with questions.

Dan Benson spoke at last.

"You and Kevin both know the dogs will be leaving us soon, right?" he asked quietly.

Tessa nodded, her face suddenly forlorn.

"But you don't know that once Larkin goes, Kevin will be leaving too. He's going to live with his aunt and uncle. They were in Ireland when his parents split up, but they are back now and eager to have him. I think it will be just right for him. He doesn't know yet. They are coming to visit first in two or three weeks."

"Oh," Tessa muttered, staring at the ground. Her hair fell down to hide her face.

The man cleared his throat and turned toward her.

"But there is something else for you to consider," he said gruffly. "Peg and I have decided to give up being foster parents after he goes, but we would like to have a child to keep. For years, we've been letting each child go to people wanting to adopt. We are both very fond of you, and we have learned that your father made you available for adoption. If you are willing, we would like to apply to adopt you. This would make you our daughter for life instead of our foster child."

He looked away and cleared his throat again. Shakespeare knew he was nervous. Tessa looked stunned.

"Think about it, honey. There's no rush. I told Peg I'd sound you out. But you can say no."

Shakespeare wanted to laugh. The man was not sure what Tessa would say.

Shakespeare was sure. His tail swung in great happy swoops.

His girl gasped. And her eyes widened. "Are you…kidding?" she said, her voice shaking. "You wouldn't joke about…"

"Of course I'm not kidding," he said, beginning to grin.

"I don't need to think," Tessa cried. "It would be my dream come true."

"We'll go for it then," he said, gently tugging a handful her hair. "You've grown on us since you came stamping into our lives. Now we can't get along without you."

He reached one long arm around her shoulders and gave her a quick hug. Tessa leaned against him until he let go and started to walk on down the path. She was so filled with astonished joy that she did not move for a moment. Then she rushed after him, taking great leaps and skips in her delight.

They were on their way home when the glory of the day was spoiled all in one second.

Crack! A sound like a pistol shot shattered the silence. Dan Benson stared up as Tessa jumped in shock. Before either of them had time to run, a great limb that had been weakened by the storm broke away from the trunk of one of the big old trees and plummeted down, just missing Tessa but striking Daniel Benson, knocking him to the earth. When the noise of its falling ceased, the woods were uncannily silent, and the man on the ground, with blood running from a cut on his head and the branch pinning him down, lay as still as death.

Chapter 10

Rescue Pup

"Dad!" Tessa cried, dropping to her knees.

It was the first time Shakespeare had heard such anguish in her voice, but her foster father did not stir. Tessa's face was chalk white and her eyes grew huge with terror.

"Oh, if only Mom were here!" she sobbed, clutching his limp hand.

She had let the leash fall. She needed help. Shakespeare knew he must not delay. He gave one big bark, strong and confident.

I'll be quick, that bark said.

Her head jerked around automatically. She saw him. Hoping she had understood, he sped off to fetch help.

He leaped over fallen logs and ducked under trailing branches. Halfway home, his leash snagged on a rock. He pulled it free. Then the flying leather loop snagged on a fence post. The dog tugged. The leash held fast.

He whimpered. Then he stopped himself. If he understood humans, he should be able to think like one. It took a split second to see the trouble. He backed up and rose on his hind legs. Using his nose, he pushed the loop up until it slipped over the top of the post.

He was off again. Then he skidded to a halt. Right in front of him rushed the creek, swollen from the rain, deep enough to drown a dog, the creek of his nightmares, the water where he had come close to death.

How could he have forgotten?

They had crossed it earlier, but Tessa had been right in front of him so he had

felt safe. How could he do it alone? He couldn't.

You wanted to do one grand thing for Tessa. This is your chance, he yelled at himself. *GO!*

He closed his eyes, gave a gulp like a sob and, ears flying, bolted across the plank bridge, which bounced under his pounding paws. He raced on.

Mrs. Benson was in the garden. He sailed over the low fence she had put around her plants and landed next to her, panting hard.

"Shakespeare, what on earth are you doing here?" she demanded, staring at him. Since she was kneeling, they were eye to eye. She read in his pleading gaze his desperate need for her to come.

"Okay, boy," she said, scrambling up. "What's wrong?"

Shakespeare tore over to the back door and pawed at it so hard that he left claw marks in the wood. She would need the box she always got when one of them was hurt, the one with bandages in it.

Hurry, he longed to shout at her. *Hurry!*

"What on earth...?" she began. Then she knew. "The First Aid box. I hear you," she said and ran into the house. She was out in seconds, clutching the box in her arms. He dashed ahead of her, pausing every so often to make sure she was not flagging.

"I'm right behind you," she panted. "Keep going, boy."

They were at the creek. He stopped dead and waited for her to catch up and go ahead. She was startled. He had been the leader ever since he had leaped over the garden fence. But there was no time to waste in wondering why. She gave him one questioning look and hurried across the plank bridge. He pushed so close behind her that she was almost thrown off balance.

"Watch out, dog," she ordered him, springing ahead to reach solid ground and safety. She did not notice that he had not once looked down at the water, tumbling just beneath his paws. Seconds after Mrs. Benson made it across, Tessa's dog bounded up the bank and took the lead once more. He plunged down the pathway into the bush. He never paused to wonder whether or not he knew the way. Instinct drew him straight back to where Daniel Benson lay white and still, close to an ancient maple with one limb snapped off. Tessa knelt next to the body, her face bloodless, her wide eyes fixed on him as she prayed for any sign of life.

"We're here," Peg Benson called to her breathlessly. "Has he moved or said anything?"

Tessa had eased the large branch off of her foster father's body and she was holding a wad of tissue tight against the cut on his head. But that was all, and it had taken every bit of her courage.

"Oh, Mom, how did you know?" she cried, her white face full of relief.

"Your blessed dog," the woman said. "He even told me to bring the First Aid box."

"Shakespeare to the rescue!" the girl said. "I was afraid he'd been scared by the tree falling and just run off."

"Not he. Oh, your father just blinked. You're all right, Dan. Don't try to move. Tessa, go and call Dr. Barnabas. I'll stay. Take your wonder dog."

"Come on, Rescue Pup," Tessa shouted joyfully.

With her keeping him safe, Shakespeare braved the creek crossing without betraying his terror. Rescue Pup! He liked the sound of that.

Tessa and he waited for what seemed like years for the ambulance to arrive. The two paramedics followed them into the woods and carried Mr. Benson out, strapped to a stretcher. He began by trying to sit up, but he fainted away, and when he came to he did what he was told.

Tessa and Kevin went along to the hospital, but the dogs, much to their disgust, had to wait at the house. It took hours. Mr. Benson had a gash on his forehead, a broken collarbone, a concussion and some bad bruises.

"I feel as though I've broken every bone in my body," he complained. But at his insistence they let him come home with them that night.

As he mended, some of the deepest hurts hidden in Tessa began to heal too. Martha waited an extra week before she came to get the dogs.

On the last night, Tessa broke the rules and let Shakespeare sleep on her bed. She stroked his velvet ears and put her cheek against his face. Shakespeare twisted around to lick her cheek and nose. He believed in wet noses.

"You're like a foster child," she told him. "You have to move on tomorrow. Fresh starts can be good though. Think if I'd never met you or the Bensons."

Then Tessa lifted his floppy ear and murmured into it, "I said I couldn't love you. I hate bawling, so I won't cry tomorrow, but I do love you with all my heart."

Shakespeare wagged his tail. If only he could speak Human for five minutes... But she understood—he could tell by the hug she gave him that nearly broke him in two.

In spite of her resolve, Tessa cried her eyes out the next day. She was Stoneface no longer.

"I can't bear to lose him," she sobbed.

"Child, you are getting him all worried," Mrs. Benson said. "Come on. This special time with him is over. You both have matured so much. Remember the day he came?"

"I told him I didn't want him," the girl wailed.

Everyone laughed.

"He knows better now," Dan Benson said. "I think he knew better from the first moment."

Tessa nodded, her tears flowing faster. Kevin rubbed his sleeve across his face and stared over her head so he wouldn't break down too.

"Well, now your Rescue Pup is ready to grow into Rescue Dog. You have to let him go. Kevin too."

Tessa wiped her face with the back of her hand. Then she took the tissue Martha held out and blew her nose long and hard.

"Okay," she said. "Go for it, Shakespeare. Make us proud, boy."

"In you go, fellows," Martha said, patting the two open cages in the back of the station wagon. The dogs hopped in.

"You'll see them again, I promise," Martha told the grieving children. "You've done a wonderful job with them. Think about taking a new pup. No, not today. But think about it."

Shakespeare had planned to comfort Larkin but, as they pulled away, he was too busy looking back at his girl. Labs have soft hearts, and he was a Lab through and through. If he had known how to weep, there would have been a flood inside the Seeing Eye car.

What will happen to us now? Larkin asked, quivering.

I'm not sure, Shakespeare told him. *They said something about our going to school.*

What's "school"? Larkin whined, no wag left in his tail.

I'm not sure of that either, Shakespeare said. *"A new adventure,"* Mrs. B. told Tessa.

But even though he was answering Larkin, he was only half listening. He was staring back at his girl who was waving and waving. His tail tried to wave back, but it was too much to ask.

The car turned out of the drive and joined the traffic on the road. He could not see Tessa any longer. Then, even the house was shut away behind trees.

Martha had promised though. "You will see them again," she had said. Holding to that promise, Shakespeare turned and faced forward, waiting for the new adventure to begin.

Jean Little is one of Canada's most beloved writers for children. She is also blind and currently living with her third Seeing Eye dog. Three times she has traveled to the Seeing Eye in New Jersey to train with a dog—first Zephyr, then Ritz and now Pippa. For years she thought about writing a book about the training of a guide-dog puppy. Now she has done it, but Shakespeare is not just any dog. Jean is also the author of *Birdie for Now* (Orca, 2002) and *I Gave My Mom a Castle* (Orca, 2003).

Orca Young Readers

Orca Young Readers Series

Max and Ellie series by Becky Citra:
*Ellie's New Home, The Freezing Moon,
Danger at The Landings, Runaway*

TJ series by Hazel Hutchins:
*TJ and the Cats, TJ and the Haunted House,
TJ and the Rockets*

Basketball series by Eric Walters:
*Three on Three, Full Court Press, Hoop Crazy!
Long Shot, Road Trip, Off Season, Underdog*

Kaylee and Sausage series by Anita Daher
Flight from Big Tangle and
Flight from Bear Canyon